Polly's Little Kite

Story and illustrations
by
Brian Maunder

New City Press
of the Focolare
Hyde Park, New York

Published in the United States by New City Press
202 Comforter Blvd., Hyde Park, NY 12538
www.newcitypress.com

Cover design by Brian Maunder
Illustrations by Brian Maunder

ISBN 978-1-56548-528-0

Printed in the United States

For Ricki and Jacob

One day, Polly and Dad made a kite.

Polly painted some fabric red and green.

Dad tied two sticks together to make a cross.

Then they put it all together.

Polly named it Little Kite.

Little Kite did not like
the big heavy cross.

"This won't help me fly"
he thought.

Polly and Dad took Little Kite to the park.

Polly held the string and Little Kite began to fly.

Whoosh. The wind blew and blew and blew.

Soon the wind was so strong that Little Kite could not hold on.

"Snap!" went the string and Little Kite flew away, higher and higher into the sky.

Polly cried when Little Kite flew away.

Little Kite flew over houses and trees.

Little Kite flew over dangerous seas.

Little Kite flew through storms and lightning.

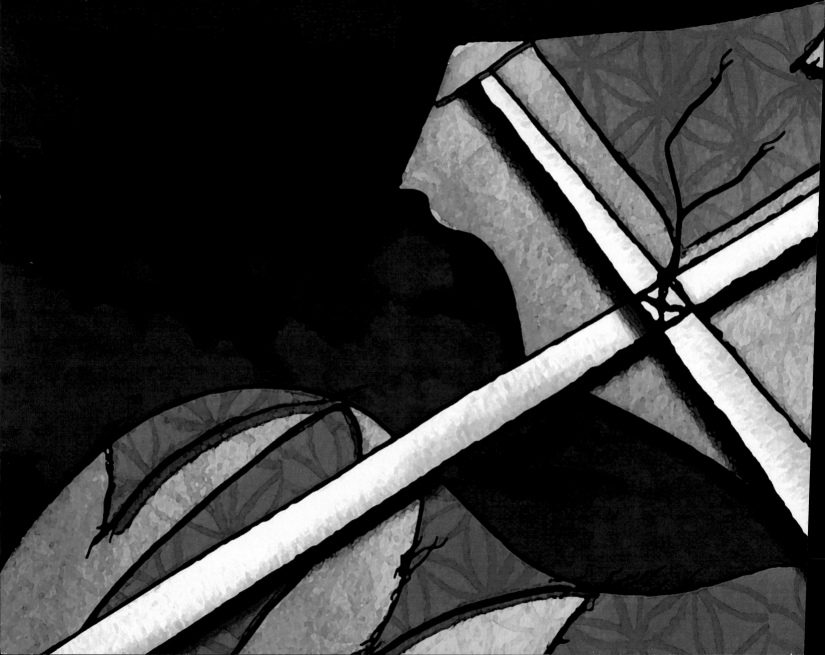

His fabric began to tear and flap in the wind.

Soon he could not fly any more and began to fall.

Then Little Kite landed
in a tree.

His tail got tangled in
the branches.

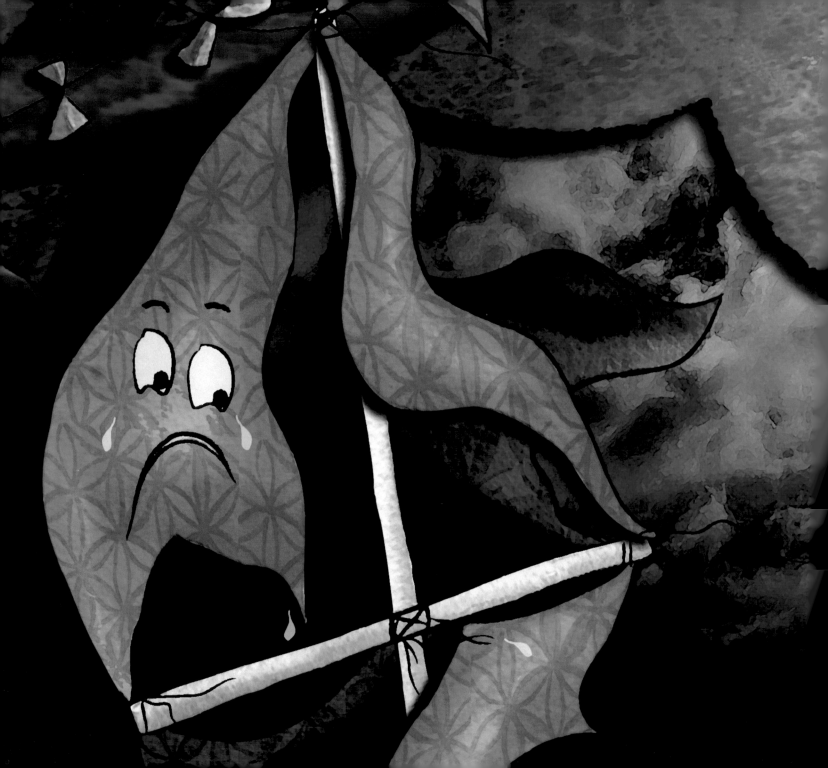

He was tattered and torn, lost and all alone.

Little Kite missed Polly.

Many days and nights passed.

One afternoon Polly and Dad went for a walk together.

As they walked, Polly looked up and saw something high up in a tree. What could it be?

"Daddy!" yelled Polly.
"There's Little Kite.
Look!"

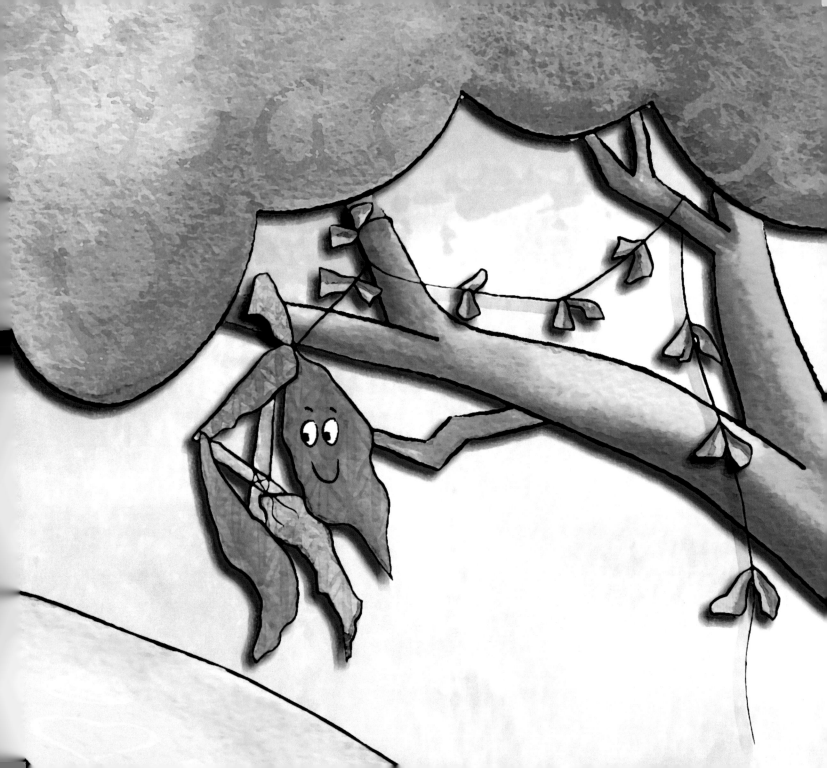

Dad climbed the tree
and pulled Little Kite
free from the branches.

"Yes! It is Little Kite!" said Polly's father.

"The tail and some fabric are still joined to the cross. If the cross had not been so strong, Little Kite would have been broken and lost forever."

"I'm so glad the cross is so strong" said Polly.

"Yes" said the father, "and with the cross we can make Little Kite new again."

Polly and Dad then repaired Little Kite together.

Little Kite was so happy.

That night, as the stars sparkled in the sky, Polly dreamed of being a beautiful kite, holding onto the cross and flying free.

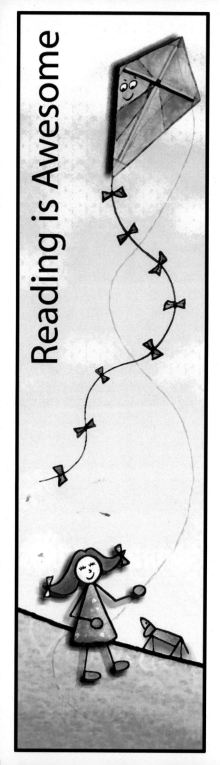

Reading is Awesome

Brian Maunder worked in sales and manufacturing for more than 15 years before making the choice to be a stay-at-home dad. Having enjoyed many years helping his children grow, he is now working in education. At work or at home, Brian has always been passionately creative in the areas of music and design. Polly's Little Kite is his first children's book.

Brian lives with his wife and 2 children in Adelaide, Australia.

How to make your own Little Kite

1. Get two straws and cut one to make it shorter than the other.

2. Join the straws together using a rubber band.

3. Thread some string up through the centre of the middle straw, leaving some out for the tail of the kite. Then bend the string down from the top of the straw and thread it through the rubber band.

4. Place the cross on some paper and trace a line from straw to straw to make a diamond kite shape. Cut out your kite shape, then draw an awesome kite design on the paper and decorate it.

5. Sticky tape the cross to your awesome design.

6. Tie some ribbon, fabric or little pieces of paper to your string to make a tail.

7. Now it's time to flyyyyyy.

NEW CITY PRESS
of the Focolare
Hyde Park, New York

About New City Press of the Focolare

New City Press is one of more than 20 publishing houses sponsored by the Focolare, a movement founded by Chiara Lubich to help bring about the realization of Jesus' prayer: "That all may be one" (John 17:21). In view of that goal, New City Press publishes books and resources that enrich the lives of people and help all to strive toward the unity of the entire human family. We are a member of the Association of Catholic Publishers.

Further Reading
All titles are available from New City Press.

www.NewCityPress.com

Irene the Elephant
    978-1-56548-450-4 $9.95

La Cometita De Polly (this same book in Spanish)
    978-1-56548-545-7 $11.95

Scan to join our mailing list for discounts and promotions or go to

www.newcitypress.com

and click on
"join our email list."

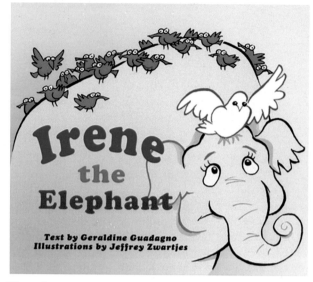

"Irene is an enormous elephant who learns that God loves her enormously – and He made her that way for a purpose. This is a beautifully written and engaging story that will touch the hearts of children and adults alike!"

Patricia Mitchell
Editorial Director,
The Word Among Us Press and
author of *Living as a Beloved Daughter of God*

Other Material of Interest

available at www.livingcitymagazine.com
The Cube of Love and *The Cube of Peace*
(starting at $7.95)

The Cubes are a simple, innovative way to transform individual behavior and group dynamics into harmonious reciprocal relations that foster universal brotherhood. Children learn how to resolve conflicts and create a new culture based on mutual respect and concern becoming co-builders of peace.

Living City Magazine

A magazine that shows that unity is possible among diverse people in many circumstances of everyday life.